Tips for Reading Together

Children learn best when reading is fun.

- Talk about the title and the pictures on the cover.
- Look through the pictures together and discuss what you think the story might be about.
- Read the story together, pointing to the words and inviting your child to join in.
- Give lots of praise as your child reads with you, and help them when necessary.
- Have fun finding the hidden cats.
- Enjoy re-reading the story and encourage your child to say the repeated phrases with you.

Children enjoy reading stories again and again. This helps to build their confidence.

Have fun!

Find the cat hidden in every picture.

Super Dad!

Written by Roderick Hunt
Illustrated by Alex Brychta

OXFORD

UNIVERSITY PRESS

"Look at Dad," said Mum.

"Dad looks silly," said Wilma.

"No, he looks good," said
Wilf.

Dad put on a red nose.

"Oh!" said Wilma.

"Dad looks so silly."

Dad had a bucket.

"Put your money in here,"
he said.

Oh no! A man took Dad's money.

"Stop!" called Mum. "Come back."

But the man didn't stop.

Dad got on a bike.

The man ran fast . . .

but Dad went faster.

"Got you," said Dad.

"Help!" said the man.

"Super Dad!" said Wilma.

Think about the story

Why did Wilma say that Dad looked silly?

What happened after the man took the bucket?

How did Dad stop the thief?

What would you like to dress up as?

A maze

Help Dad to catch the thief.

More books for you to enjoy

Level 1: Getting Ready

Level 2: Starting to Read

Level 3: Becoming a Reader

Level 4: Building Confidence

Level 5: Reading with Confidence

OXFORD
UNIVERSITY PRESS

Great Clarendon Street,
Oxford OX2 6DP

Text © Roderick Hunt 2006
Illustrations © Alex Brychta 2006

First published 2006
All rights reserved

Series Editors: Kate Ruttle,
Annemarie Young

British Library Cataloguing
in Publication Data available

ISBN–13: 978-019-279228-0

10 9 8 7 6 5 4 3

Printed in China by Imago

Have more fun with Read at Home